FEMALE WARRIORS

THE RISE

JAYA RAM

Dedicated to Sri Sri MahaPeriyava

Contents

Preface

I was born in an orthodox family doing business for more than five decades studied Commerce in Sri Vasavi College, Erode. Marketing was my job, writing affection base verses is my all time passion but never published. Travelling more places meeting new faces chat with new minds is my lifetime favorite. Writing novel in my own style was created in my mind when I met a bold girl author in a train travel some years ago. I will meet YOU in more Fiction and Non-fiction books in near future.

Jaya Ram
The Author

Acknowledgements

I thank everyone for making this book published. I thank God for being with me allover my life.

Jaya Ram

The Author

Prologue

If you go for a consultation with a General Doctor for illness, what you expect from the Doctor? The Cure! But some of them give you a big shock by stealing the valuable from your body. They took blood and the organ without your knowledge. How do you react? Here is a story with extreme shock. Find the thrill all over the work. Enjoy and leave a comment to the under mentioned mail id. You will receive surprise gifts for selected comments too.

The Author.<rajatheauthor22@gmail.com>

CHAPTER ONE

Murder Trial

I am trying to open the bed room door knob. Door inside locked.

Who is inside?

Question rolled in my mind.

After some tricky trials, door opened.

I have opened the door slowly.

Cooler is running. Fan also.

A young girl was lying in well decorated bed covered by flowered bed- linen, as shot and bleed.

She seems like a fairy queen drawing work by Picaso.

"Ms.Pavithra, still you are not yet prepared for the function, why making so delay my friend?" ask Nandhini and continues, "6 PM function, already it is nearing 7 PM, why you are making so late?

"Just few minutes," said Pavithra locked apartment door and came out with Nandhini.

"Let's go". They went by cab.

Before they reach the function hall, few lines about them.......

Pavithra just now joined in that IT company which located in outskirts of the city with B.Tech graduation with lots of professional dreams. Nandhini is her team mate and friend with same energy waves. Pavithra's family is farm based. Single daughter, intelligent, bold youth and low spending hands.

\-

After paying the cab, they enter the venue, enquired the receptionist about the function hall and moved into.

Well perfumed simply decorated hall. Music waved in air. Co staff Mr.Aravind-Malini marriage reception going on with camera flash lights

After presenting gift to the staff, posing for camera, they came to buffet. After finish up with light food they came out by saying bye-bye to the new couples and caught the cab.

They reached Pavithra's apartment by 9PM

"Already it's too late, stay with me tonight my friend you may go straightly to work from here tomorrow "said Pavithra, then Nandhini accepted.

Mobile ringed missed and wake them up," its new number" said Nandhini .

Pavithra called that number.

"Ms.Pavithra, this is Ashok"

Which Ashok, question rolled on mind,

"Tell me, you.....?

"Yesterday... at function hall... I gave you tissue paper..."Ashok

"It's ok, then what Mr.?"

"How did you know my number", she asked again

"I found your card in your Hand bag, you missed in function hall chair" he said

"Oh!, sorry and thanks, how can I collect from you?

"By 10 O'clock in front of office" he said

"My office?" she asked

"Yes" Ashok finished.

"Ok Ok" Pavithra closed the conversation.

Ashok expecting Pavithra at her office entrance by said time. "Mr. Ashok...?"

"Yes, Ms. Pavithra"

She collected the handbag and willing to move by saying "Thanks "to Ashok

"Are you saying that's all?" Ashok continued

"Then what? Expecting any money from me?" tensed Pavithra

"No, Just a coffee with me once?" Ashok replied with eager to continue the relationship

"See Mr.Ashok, I said thanks for the timely help, I don't want to continue the relationship, Ok, let me go?" Pavithra replied with little stiff in voice and continued to go inside her office without waiting for his next reply.

After some days,

"What happen Driver? Pavithra asked cab driver when he slowed the car.

Driver stopped the car and went to know what happened amidst of the crowd of peoples gathered.

"A small accident madam, this old lady lying down in road, shall you please drop us in my clinic..." asked that young man with an old lady brought by him and cab driver.

Pavithra replied excitedly after seeing Dr.Ashok is that young man and said "Yes, let's go"

They dropped at Dr.Ashok's Clinic and went to her office

Nandhini asked Pavithra after she saw the difference in the face of Pavithra

"What happened?'

Pavithra narrated the incident

"Anything important?" Nandhini asked again.

"Don't dream about Ashok, I have no idea about nothing"

"It's ok, I won't ask you again" Nandhini dropped the conversation.

When a new number ringed, Pavithra got tensed, after seeing no one notice her conversation, asked

"Tell me"

"Shall you able to give that recorded pen drive this weekend?"

"Yes, Sir" replied in husky voice and put the phone.

/-

That said Saturday came.

"Ms.Pavithra, shall we go for shopping today, asked Nandhini.

"Ok Ms.Nandhini, we go by evening" Pavithra said.

By 4PM evening after had coffee with little snacks in office canteen, they started by cab for shopping by dropping permission request to the Team Head.

They entered that mall

Nandhini bought shoes and next they went to cosmetic section.

One guy wearing blue jerkin came near to Pavithra and showed his palm without showing face to Nandhini.

Expected pavithra gave that pen drive which she kept hidden in her hand bag and that guy gone out from that scene quickly.

“Ms.Pavithra, amount transferred to your account” said that phone call.

Pavithra accepted that private deal as she thought the subject will be used for a good cause, as she doesn’t know their real character.

/-

One rainy dawn without season, the time is 06.30 morning

Phone rings,

“Who is there?”

“Pavithra, this is Ashok”

“Tell me” she not interested to reply

“I ask you straightly Ms.Pavithra, shall you able to accept me as your friend?”

“Sorry Mr. Ashok, I don’t like” she replied

“Don’t you like me?”

“No, I don’t like to add anyone as my male friend at all”

“Will you please stop calling me again?” Pavithra with little anger

“Ok Ms.Pavithra, I won’t disturb you hereafter” Ashok closed the call.

\-

“Ms Pavithra, my mother is coming from my hometown, shall I pickup and go to my room now?” Nandhini asked

“Ok my friend you carry on. I have some work pending” Pavithra replied tiredly.

/-

Nandhini’s phone call waked up next day morning.

“Ms Pavithra, my mother got some health disturbances today. Bringing her to hospital today and afternoon I will join you. Shall you able to manage our table work and will you inform Team head regarding my half day permission?"

"Oh sure, update me about her health after consulting the physician."Pavithra added " I shall inform Team head"

When waiting for consultation Nandhini read the name of Doctor. The board spells as "Dr. Ashok Rajarathnam. M.B., B.S., MD (Gen)

There was no necessity happened to her to consult this doctor even his clinic is near to her apartment.

When her turn came she gone inside with her mother

After all questions answered by her mother Dr. wrote some medicines in his prescription slip and narrated the health condition and tablets to be consumed

When Nandhini started to came she asked " Mr Ashok , you the person mean by MsPavithra?"

"Yes of course, I am that unlucky person" replied Ashok, added "she has not accept me as just a friend even"

"She is reserved type guy. Don't mistake her" Nandhini replied and noted his smile has some attraction and her mind warned her he is some dangerous person to handle.

CHAPTER TWO

Cross Talk

Amidst of her work schedule, Pavithra has recorded that cross talk. That conversation includes transfer of datas, lab codes some related to blood donors

“How your mother is now “asked Pavithra

“Doctor referred some medicines, still fever not yet balanced, evening I have to consult the Dr again

With no reason Nandhini forget to say that Doctor is Mr Ashok

When Pavithra working in office data base a phone call interrupted. It’s from a new number. Time 11 AM

“Ms Pavithra?”

“Yes, you..?”

“Your Team head Jegan”

“Yes sir, Tell me sir, anything Important?

“Shall we meet at our office canteen now? Are you busy?”

“No sir shall we.”

In canteen...

“Take coffee Ms.Pavithra”

“Oh sure, anything unofficial?”

“No, But nowadays you are always in tension mood, any health problem? Added

“Your report shows weak this week” Jegan

“No sir I am normal, why sir?”

“I have noticed some phone call disturb you, you are often going to the entrance of our office and meeting some person” added “Have you engaged any affair or any alliance fixed?” Jegan straightly crossed the eyes of Ms.Pavithra.

"No sir, nothing serious," and narrated the hand bag missing and collected from Dr.Ashok.

"It's ok; whatever may be just inform me, I will sure help you" Mr.Jegan way back to cabin with Pavithra

"Any problem?" Nandhini asked

Pavithra replied as it is.

Pavithra warned herself to be careful and some eyes are watching in office

/-

Pavithra just relaxed after a simple face wash in room and sat in sofa and scrolling news channel.

Phone rings..

"Ms Pavithra my mother want to see you, shall we come to meet you now?" Nandhini

"Oh sure, welcome" said and put the phone.

Pavithra made little fresh up and searched whether any snacks in Dining table.

Hope they will reach in 20-30 minutes; I shall order in swiggy now, thinking Pavithra and took the phone to order some food.

Calling bell rings.....

She wonders how fast they came and opened the door.

A small boy from next door and told "Aunty this post for you"

After some minutes,

Nandhini came with her mother.

Her mother told Pavithra, "We have got good alliance for Nandhini and it seems most of family points matching us" added "We most probably planning to conduct marriage in two months itself"

"Wow, good news from you, Nandhini, advance congrats"

"But why you didn't inform me" Pavithra asked Nandhini

"Just now mother confirmed this alliance first of all you are the person to inform at once"

"Ok don't be lazy prepare for the function, call me for the shopping dress and jewels whatever may be, I will join you sure"

After they went Pavithra opened the post and got excited. After her graduation she had done a specialized PG course. She wondered about the Grade mentioned as "A" in her PG Certificate.

\-

After joined this company one fine morning....

Amidst of client calling from data base, one cross talk she heard. When she like to avoid and overcome that crank call, the conversation was some interesting topic is going on between doctors and the topic is related to Organ donate, after some minutes line hanged.

"Pavithra, mother asked shall we go for shopping today." Nandhini

"Today I have some important work in office, shall we by 4PM tomorrow?" Pavithra.

The same cross talk often crossing Pavithra's work. With some intention strikes Pavithra recorded the cross talk continuously....

In a famous Textile shop Nandhini searched pure silk, soft silk, fancy bhutta and double warp something related to sarees. But Pavithra's eyes were noticed that Blue jerkin guy.

After payment made for the purchases and came out of the shop, there was cloudy climate and choice of rain starts.

"Nandhini, shall we continue shopping tomorrow? Pavithra

"Hmm. Ok, we shall" replied Nandhini and called the cab

That blue jerkin guy came near to Pavithra, dropped a small piece of paper to Pavithra and vanished fast

After dropped Pavithra at her apartment, Nandhini returned with her mother

That small slip told to meet some person at 8 AM IBBI Bank, located at Sarakki Lake

Thinking who that person is, Pavithra consumed some food and went to sleep.

\-

"You are so cute Ms Nandhini" Dr.Ashok told her 100th time. Some attraction in Ashok locked Nandhini in a friendship. They had break-fast at a restaurant way to suratkal beach and they went by

Ashok's car.

/-

"Driver, go to JP nagar" Pavithra called the cab added the time and place to pick her up

After heard the spot, driver told "I will be there madam and we shall reach the place in 20 minutes"

That same blue jerkin guy she saw in front of IBBI Bank

"Second floor madam" he told

In front of the Aircondioned room.

The name plate spells Mr.Edwin..Zonal Manager, DSA Accounts.

"Tell me Mr Edwin"added "Why you called me so early?"

Edwin got irritated when Pavithra called him with name and thinking that he had to avoid controversy, "Ms Pavithra you are the main reason to start a new project with our doctor friends, and more over the details in cross talk will be very much helpful to us" added

"Please sit down madam" he ordered a coffee for her. The assistant gave coffee from Nescafe vending Machine

She had some sips and put the coffee cup in table and asked Edwin "Tell me sir,"

"As we need some more details, will you please continue recording that cross talk communications,?"

"Sorry sir, there are more hurdles in our office to record the communication, I will do once and after that don't call me please" Pavithra concluded and started to go back.

"Ms.Pavithra, mother is going back to hometown for the preparation work and Invitation printing, I am going to drop her in Airport. Shall you please inform our Team Head?"Nandhini

"Oh sure, I will inform"

When Pavithra prepared to close the calling clients, the cross talk started

This time the content gave shock feel and took some seconds to understand the seriousness of the conversation.

Pavithra went to washroom and sprayed water in face to fresh up and back to her seat and again heard the recorded conversation and decided not to give recorded pen drive to that team.

CHAPTER THREE

Crime Trial

"Sorry Mr.Ashok" Nandhini replied when Mr.Ashok invited to his house to stay with her this night. Nandhini added that her marriage was arranged and hereafter she won't come with Mr.Ashok anywhere and also came today only to inform this to him. Ashok disappointed with her reply and planned somewhere have to enjoy her. He sadly said, "Ok Ms Nandhini let's go"

By the way to his car he asked Nandhini "sure, are you invite me for your Marriage?'

Nandhini replied "Yes of course" there seems some hurry in her walk to escape from the scene.

/-

"Shall I send my guy this evening, Ms.Pavithra?" Edwin's friend in a overseas call

Pavithra replied in strict voice "Sorry sir, I can't record the content. There were more questions in my office, don't call me again" she hanged the phone.

Nandhin told Pavithra that Mr.Ashok invited her to his house. Pavithra concludes "All guys have same thoughts"

When Pavithra prepared to sleep, Phone rings up. "Ms.Pavithra, please handover the recorded content" The voice is from Edwin irritated her.

"Sorry sir, hereafter don't disturb me, ok?"

\-

"I have to apply for a long leave in our office probably by next week" Nandhini added "I have to help my mother for the marriage preparations"

"Wow, merry Queen, do you remember me to invite?" Pavithra asked her

Nandhini "Sorry madam we won't let you so easy, you have to accompany with my family for all the days the function conducted" added " I will arrange for the flight tickets for you also, ok?" and questioned her "Are you sure coming to attend?"

"Oh, definitely I will" Pavithra.

/-

Pavithra started some minutes early to inform to the Police department after she heard some serious conversation in cross talk.

Pavithra noted Nandhini as she seems to be something disturbed and asked

"What happen Ms. Nandhini?"

"Morning eat some dosa of which prepared from ready mix batter, my stomach not well". She urged to run to washroom at once.

Pavithra followed her

After some minutes Nandhini came back to seat denoted that she is affected from food poison.

Pavithra recommended her to consult a doctor nearby soon and advised to take rest afternoon

They both informed Team Head and went to a hospital, Pavithra dropped Nandhini in her apartment after consulted the doctor and started to go back office. The time is 12 noon

/-

Pavithra guided the cab driver as "Driver, please drop me near Sri Saran Bank".

Driver "it is one way madam, I have to turn the ring road and will reach there soon" replied

There was more crowd and busy in South Division office. She suddenly noted that a young man who got down from the Police vehicle, that one is Dr.Ashok

Nandhini get down from the cab and delayed some minutes let Dr Ashok may go from the scene.

Dr Ashok came back from that office in few minutes and went by a two wheeler driven by someone.

She paid the cab charges and entered the office. She enquired the crossed PC about DC sir cabin

Nandhini called her, " Pavithra I feel drowsy and worried to be alone, shall I be with you tonight?" She replied "Yes and come."

Middle aged DC Mr.Somnath invited her and showed the chair in front of him to sit

"Ok, Lawyer Mr.Sankar and silviya, let's discuss the murder case tomorrow itself" said to the official persons already occupied the adjacent seats and turned his face to Pavithra and asked "Tell me madam"

She narrated from the beginning as there cross talk started, after some calls she called the person to know that there is cross talk she heard in my work between calls and to check the connection they communicate every time

But the reason is to erase the crime proof, they want the recording details of which Pavithra missed to notice.

DC Mr.Somnath told the real reason they asked the recording details from her.

Pavithra thought she came in right time to DC sir.

DC.Somnath said "If I involve at this stage they will escape, I will introduce a person to you, you just say actually what happened, to that person, and she will take care of your case"

Pavithra collected the name and contact details of that person and said," Sir, I have to meet my friend at once as she is in critic health issue and then I will inform the person everything"

DC Sir said"Ok, you carry on"

Pavithra called the cab and said to go to her office. She got a overseas phone call and the voice in that call warned her for informing everything to Police moreover added that they know how to collect the recorded device from her.

After a second, Pavithra back to form herself.

/-

After informing the cab driver regarding her office land mark Pavithra called Nandhini, ring goes non-stop, but there was no response. She thought that she might be in serious condition

"Please wait for some minutes" said to the cab driver and walked in to her office. She take some important things from her cabin including 'That' material and came out.

Cab went to Nandhini's apartment. Pavithra stepped little running to the lift and pressed to first floor.

She reached Nandhini's room no 11 and pressed the bell.

\-

"Hai, My name is Sancheti Rawat, DC Mr. Somnath told to talk with you" Pavithra received a call from Ms.Sancheti and assumed she must be well trained Army Personnel.

Pavithra narrated to Sancheti as told to DC Mr.Somnath when she was in travel.

"Shall we meet once" Sancheti asked

"Sure, but I am in a hurry to meet my friend, she was in ill condition. After I reach my apartment I call you" Pavithra replied.

When there was no response, Pavithra get down from first floor and went to adjacent mini coffee bar and took some cutlet and coffee as she felt the need of this minute.

/-

"Ms.Pavithra, shall we meet at your apartment today?" sancheti asked again.

Pavithra replied "Yes madam we will meet by 4PM"

"Ok, we will meet then" Sancheti concluded

Pavithra called DC Mr. Somnath and said she is about to meet Ms.Sancheti and asked "Shall she reliable and am I narrate everything to her?"

"Ms.Pavithra, Ms.Sancheti was trained in Army school and she was belongs to the best batch of 2016 in Dehradun IMA South camp" and added "Tell her and she will handle everything"

"Ok, Thank you sir" Pavithra replied hopefully.

\-

After finished emergency calls and reporting work in office cabin, Pavithra called Nandhini twice, but no response.

Sancheti called Ms.Pavithra

“Ms.Pavithra, I have informed you about our meeting by 4PM, shall I?”

“Yes Madam” told Pavithra and sent her apartment location word through ‘What3 words’ app.

Ms.Sancheti stood gently in front of Pavithra’s apartment block doorstep, wearing formal suit covered with Black Jerkin.

Pavithra brought her to her apartment

Her door not locked.

There was Nandhini’s shoe in front of her apartment

She moved into her apartment with Ms.Sancheti and found Nandhini’s handbag in sofa.

Pavithra called “Nandhini” and going to her bedroom, it was locked inside

CHAPTER FOUR

Life Saved

Then in the voice of Ms.Sancheti,

"I am trying to open the door, it was inside locked.

"I am trying to open the door with my small blade like blind keys from my blades bunch from my jerkin inner packet. After some tricky trial moves, door opened.

The cooler and Ceiling fan was running. One young girl lying in a well flowered printed bed-linen, seems to be shot and looks like a water sprayed Picaso's Art painting.

Pavithra went near and shouting "Nandhini"

Sancheti stopped her and advised not to touch anything in the room and checked the pulse of Nandhini.

Soon in seconds took her phone and commanded her team members fast.

Then check and round the bed saw a man lying in bathroom with blood in left wrist and held by right hand and fell down unconsciously.

The window without any cross bars was kept opened. Ms.Sancheti check over that window saw a man with blue jerkin running through the adjacent road.

That man was Dr.Ashok and he was picked by ambulance attenders and gone to Dr.Ashok's clinic for emergency treatment as advised by Ms.Sancheti.

When Nandhini came to Pavithra's apartment and reached near to lift,

"Ms.Nandhini"... She jerked and turns back and saw Dr.Ashok and asked "Hey, how are you here and how did you know this apartment?"

"No, I have some work in this area, I saw you here and followed you, that's all" Dr.Ashok replied and added "Is it your Home?"

Nandhini thought her address should not be disclosed to him and said "Yes, come inside"

Ashok sat in a sofa and asked her shall you offer me a coffee, Ms.Nandhini?"

Nandhini want to take a perfect rest in Pavithra's home for at least a hour of sleep, but she hide the irritation and gone to kitchen and put the water pan in Gas stove.

After she prepared a coffee to him only and put hot water kettle in the stove.

She gave coffee to Dr.ashok and asked him, "Tell me Mr.Ashok" with question feel and she thought herself to send him out of the scene soon.

"Coffee very good" said and put the cup on the table and came very close to her.

Nandhini went little back and told him with little anger, "Please Mr.Ashok, don't misuse your influence and keep your dignity good and move back". But Ashok almost came and rounded her neck and held entire of her tight and tried to catch her pink layered lips but he was able to kiss in cheek only.

After some struggle Nandhini switched the lever from right hand second finger. A micro surgical blade came out from that lever from finger and in right position she scratched the left hand wrest vain of Mr.ashok and pulled him forcefully. Ashok lyed down slowly with bleeding in that scratched hand in Bathroom and received a blow in forehead by metal torch by Nandhini.

In a fraction of second she thanked Pavithra in mind for giving that micro blade lever wearing in finger for her personal safety.

Nandhini came back in farm and saw back after heard little sound in front room. One guy, wearing blue jerkin, searched something in her hand bag.

She stepped towards him shouting "Hey...You".

That guy ran by pushing Nandhini into bedroom.

When Nandhini again came to him, he forcibly pushed her and shot her by his gun and after he heard sounds near the entrance door, he escaped from the scene using the window and get down from the floor parapet via pipeline and ran quickly.

Nandhini fell down in the bed slowly.

/-

Ms.Sancheti smelled the gas from kitchen, ran fast there with her Magnum pistol. There was a kettle going to melting stage without water. She switched off the knob as well as the main connector and informed Pavithra "Incident happened might be within seconds" Then gone to Dr.Ashok checked the pulse rate.

Asked Pavithra some cotton cloth and bonded Ashok's hand.

Ms.Sancheti narrated to the cops and attenders .

"Ms.Sandria, Take Nandhini to GH in your own vehicle, move fast and update her health to me soon"

"Mr.Ranjith, take Dr.Ashok to his clinic and treat fast. And put some cops for not permitting Dr.Ashok going out"

"Mr.Rohan, inform this area station and control room to block and search the outgoing all vehicles"

Turn back to Ms.Pavithra and asked "Did you suspect anyone?"

After deliver all commands Ms.Sancheti went to Sarakki Lake with Ms.Pavithra in her own cab.

\-

"Ms.Pavithra, Is it Mr.Edwin , the officer you met in 2nd floor of IBBI, sarakki lake?" Sancheti asked

"Yes Madam." Pavithra replied.

When they both reached the Edwin sir room, it was locked.

Ms.Sancheti stopped the floor manager who came there and asked about Mr.Edwin

"Mr.Edwin got transfer to Pune branch and vacated his quarters today morning only"

Ms.Sancheti called Control room,

" Mr.George, Matter serious, tell your staffs to connect railway cops to block Mr.Edwin going towards Pune".

"Then inform Kempe Gowda Airpot officials to held Mr.Edwin if he is travelling by Air"

"Call local travel agency AIR ONE and find out the Airlines name Mr.Edwin booked"

(There was AIRONE name written in backside of Mr.Edwin visiting card collected from Ms.Pavithra's hand bag)

Ms.Sancheti called Local BSNL senior manager to get Mr.Edwin Mobile outgoing call statement.

She also called Dr.Ashok clinic EDP in-charge to get non patient and Dr.ashok's friends list. They initially refused to give. Dc Mr.Somnath there gave some notifications to EDP in-charge only after his call they gave the list.

Ms.Sancheti shortlisted and referred everything through her tab. Pavithra wondered about her work speed.

"Ms.Pavithra, Nandhini came out of danger. Her mother is coming from hometown, are you going to receive her mother?" Sancheti added a question that shocked Ms.Pavithra a little seconds," Ms.Pavithra, how you had got interested in studying Weapons Engineering?"

She stunned on the speed of analyzing of Ms.Sancheti.

"Ms.Pavithra, I have seen your certificates which you have studied in NewJersey" said Ms.Sancheti and also shown some photos of bullets taken from Ms.Nandhini's body.

"Shall you able to say that the bullet belongs to which gun Ms.Pavithra?"

"Is it 9mm Calibre Madam?"

"Well, you have assumed exactly" Ms.Sancheti

"Ok Ms.Pavithra, Nandhini's mother will reach airport now, you just pickup and bring her to GH please"

Pavithra called Mr.Jegan, her team head and applied leave for 2 days.

/-

Ms.Sancheti received a call from cops on duty in Dr.Ashok clinic and told that they held a person who came to meet Dr.Ashok.

"Madam, our team cops held Mr.Edwin here at Hyderabad who came by The Flight Air Asia" added "We need permission from DC Somnath Sir to bring Mr.Edwin back to Mangalore" Mr.George told to Ms.Sancheti.

Ms.Sancheti heard all cross call details by headset when going to Dr.Ashok's clinic with Pavithra.

Cab reached the clinic by 10 AM

Cops guided Ms.Sancheti to the room where the suspect guy was kept. That person wearing Blue jerkin was remembered by Ms.Sancheti as the man ran from Pavithra's apartment.

"Madam please use this table, you need any coffee?" asked the assistant in the room. Sancheti replied," Ya, I need two coffee and call Ms.Pavithra to come inside the room"

Sancheti turned to that guy, "yes, tell me mister, what's your name?"

"John Britto, tell me madam why the cops kept me here?

"Just tell me why you came here and what‘s the relationship between you and Dr.Ashok?"

"I am working in Dr.Ashok sir friend office and I will visit here often for delivering documents and collecting reports from Dr.Ashok" and added

"Why madam any problem, what happened to Dr.Ashok?"

"Yesterday why you have gone to Ms.Pavithra's apartment, tell me mr.John?"

"Pavithra...Who is she madam?"Asked Mr.John and his face is so normal even met Ms.Pavithra who entered the room that minute.

Ms.Sanchet picked the mobile from Ms.Pavithra and showed Nandhini's Photo from Mobile.

After seeing Nandhini's photo, John tried to run from there.

Ms.Pavithra slapped Mr.John's face and the speed of the action was around 1.5tonnes.

Mr.John's face turn reddish and bubbled and fallen down in the corner of the room. Ms.Pavithra picked him with his shirt collar and shown the chair to sit and relax. She gave water bottle to him to refresh.

Assistant gave coffee cups to Ms.Pavithra and Ms.Sancheti

After some minutes Ms.Pavithra asked "Mr.John, why you have tried to kill Ms.Nandhini?"

"Madam, Dr.Ashok gave me the address (Pavithra's) and to collect the pen drive from her and if she refuse to give, then told to use the gun" and added," on any account he need that device" and added "I don't know Dr.Ashok sir is there inside the room at the time and I have gone inside as he already told that the device must be inside her handbag" John replied with high fear on his face.

After a minute, John Continued, "When I enter the room that lady was fighting with someone, I found the bag there but there is no device in the bag. When she came to catch me I pulled down and shot her and finally I escaped from there."

After had some breath he added "Other than this, I don't know anything madam" His voice metered slow.

Ms.Sancheti handed over John to the cops came from DC office and told them" Please keep Mr.John in lockup and inform me if anyone came to meet him or called him via phone" Cops gone to do their duty.

Ms.Sancheti came to DR.Ashok room with Ms.Pavithra. "Mr.Ashok, you are a reputed professional, are you willing to taste the imprisonment experience?" added,

" your clinic was surrounded with our cops. Don't try to go out please as we have to enquire you once again. We shall soon come back" told Ms.Sancheti.

Ms.Sancheti came out to reception and told "Don't allow any new patient, give me your inpatient list and inform all duty staffs to go home as leave until our enquiry finish up"

The receptionist replied" there is no inpatient right now madam"

Ms.Sancheti went to DC office with Ms.Pavithra.

CHAPTER FIVE

Arrest One

Dr.Ashok's mobile phone ringed. One cop saw inside the room to know what the matter is. But Ashok replied it's a call from home. Then cop back to his seat.

"Tell me Mr.Edwin"

"Mr.Ashok, I came to Hyderabad. That lady Ms.Pavithra informed to Police about cross call matter.

Already I asked my office about my transfer but yesterday only I got the transfer copy. I have to join and report to our head office next week. But because of that lady contacted the police department I have to change my plan and came here just now.

Here all the passengers kept in Airport lounge for a formal checking" Edwin described the situation.

After the call closed, one guy came near to Mr.Edwin " Ok Mr.Edwin, you are the special guest to our office today" said Mr.Dyanesh Reddy, DSP in charge, Hyderabad city came in casual dress code, and grabbed the mobile phone from Mr. Edwin

Ms.Sancheti gone through the laptop of which brought by a cop from Hyderabad.

\-

Pavithra went to pickup Nandhini's mother from Airport and also went to her apartment to take some things along with hot water bottle for Nandhini.

There she saw two cops stood in front of her apartment in casual dress and their van parked some distance roadside. Pavithra asked "Why".

They replied “DC sir sent for your protection, madam and we shall go by our van”

Pavithra rushed to GH along with Nandhini’s mother.

Ms.Nandhin was shifted to General ward as her report showed normal.

“Mom, you please be here with Ms,Nandhini and call me if any urgency” told to Nandhini’s Mother and arranged two cops for their protection, Pavithra went to DC office with Ms.Sancheti.

On the way Ms.Sancheti called Mr.Dyanesh reddy, DSP, Hyderabad city,” DSP sir, please keep Mr.Edwin and family in retired Major Jenny sir guest house with cops for safety and collect Mr.Edwin’s Mobile and Laptop” and added “and then will you able to call me from your office sir?”

Mr.Edwin’s bad time starts with the file saved in his laptop.

\-

There were three doctors in that air-conditioned conference room and they were in very nervous and waiting for Dr.KaliCharan. There was so pin drop silence except the Rummm...sound of AC.

A Guy in perfect formal Reymond suit looks like a connoisseur, entered into the room. Suddenly all of them stood in straight. That Guy showed his hands to sit all and relax. He was a famous and leading cardiologist ,IMA Mangalore President, Dr.KaliCharan sat in his executive chair and asked “Tell me friends, anything serious?

Dr.Jacob showed hands to Dr.Amrindhar and Dr.Sukla and told “ Mr.Edwin is in police custody” and stopped conversation a while silent

“Yes my P.A. informed me but no secrets get out from him, don’t worry” said Dr.KC

“Even though...” Dr.Jacob started hopelessly.

“Let’s wait up to evening” Dr.KC replied firmly.

/-

“Ms.Sancheti, this is criminal limited case, we need local crime branch head support. I will inform DC Somnath sir formally, ok?”WC Harshvarthan.

“Ok sir” replied Ms.Sancheti.

Next day morning 07.30

“Dr.Sukla injured in an accident and injured severely. Me and Dr.Amrindhar going to the hospital within half an hour” a whatsapp message from Dr.Jacob woke up Mr.KaliCharan.

Dr.Sukla done a minor operation to a patient in a private hospital and he is on the way return to home. He met an accident on a roadside tree, due to sleepy drive.

Even though Dr.KC Team tried in all effective way, they can’t save Dr.Sukla.

Very important was two bottles of rare group blood taken from Dr.Sukla’s body and saved in KC Hospital blood bank without informing his family.

/-

“How much inward amount credited to our account this month, Mr.Jacob?” Dr.KC asked.

“Up to date, 23 million bucks Mr.KC” replied Dr.Jacob.

“Ok, we will meet again Saturday party, don’t worry” replied Dr.KaliCharan.

\-

“Mr.Soman, Mr.Edwin is house arrest at Hyderabad by DSP; shall you be able to shift Mr.Edwin and family to Mangalore?” Dr.KaliCharan asked. Mr.Soman is a contract killer.

“Shall do sir, but is it ok if there is any fire on transfer?” asked Soman.

“It’s ok, try to bring them alive” Dr.KaliCharan replied and inhaled the chill air from BMW car AC.

Mr.Edwin ‘s future was decided by the file he forget to erase from his laptop

One cop brought Mr.Edwin’s Laptop and Mobile phone from Hyderabad. Ms.Sancheti gone through the laptop to know the back support for Mr.Edwin. “Who is the black sheep?” a question was rolled in Sancheti’s mind.

There she found

List of rare blood group patients from various famous hospitals all over India

List of rare blood group patients taken from the Free medical camps conducted in various parts of India including the political and financial back ground of the patients

The financial value of rare blood group bottles in International market and their network length

Ms.Sancheti consumed huge amount of water to finish the list.

\-

Pavithra brought Nandhini and her mother to her apartment for their safety.

/-

Mr.Soman went to Hyderabad searched Jenny sir guest house and brought Mr.Edwin and family after he overcome the security by showing his gun. They rushed to Mangalore.

\-

"Ms.Sancheti, where you put Mr.Edwin and his family?" asked DC Mr.Somnath.

"They are all safe in my custody DC sir; I assumed that they shall be hijacked by someone, so I had arranged proxy for them "Replied Ms.Sancheti

/-

"Just collecting and delivering the data mentioned by Mr.Edwin is our work sir" Dr.Ashok and Mr.John told to DC

"Sir, we have to get permission from court to keep in custody of Mr.Edwin" The assistant to DC

"No, No, I think the main accused will escape, what you say Ms.Sancheti?" DC asked

"Let us put Mr.Edwin in Black room and interrogate" said Ms.Sancheti and suddenly her face gone bright after seeing the symbol and showing to DC

That's three edged weapon called "Thirisoolam" in Tamil and that weapon always presence in the hands of the Lordess Maha Kali.

One hacker came to open that folder of which saved with a password. It takes around 45 minutes to open the folder.

The file contains the list of persons at the age group of around 25 to 35.

DC remembered the names suddenly and opens his own laptop to see the file “Missing persons in last three months”

DC showed that file to Ms.Sancheti.

Ms.Sancheti shocked and saw DC sir face and Said “OMG”

50 percent of names matched with the list had in Edwin’s Laptop file

When the hacker moved from the scene he spelled the name KALI regarding the symbol.

Ms.Sancheti searched that name from list of famous doctors in India and found Dr.KaliCharan and some names started in the word “Kali”. She confirmed Dr.KaliCharan name where she saw the name in Edwin’s mobile.

/-

“Ms.Pavithra, how is Ms.Nandhini’s health?” and added, “Shall we meet in café coffee day by evening 4PM?” asked Ms.Sancheti

\-

HBBC, MG road branch manager called Ms.Sancheti “ Madam, two million bucks transfer received to Mr.Edwin sir account from a person’s account of our Mumbai Branch”

/-

“DC sir, Will you please arrange 2 cops to shift Mr.Edwin alone to Pune with us?” asked Ms.Sancheti to DC Mr.somnath.

“Oh, sure I will” DC accepted her request.

\-

“Useless fellows” fired Dr.Kalicharan to Mr.Soman, as he brought fake persons from Hyderabad. Then he sent all out of the scene.

Dr.KaliCharan called Mr.Nithin working as SI in Hyderabad DSP office as he is favorable person to him.

“Tell me sir”

“Can you able to tell me where about of Mr.Edwin and his family?”

“Sir, already you had shifted them to Mangalore by someone” Nithin replied.

"So you don't know" asked Dr.Kalicharan added that "Mr.Soman shifted fake peoples, ok, I will see" Dr.KaliCharan put the phone with irritation.

/-

Ms.Sancheti with Ms.Pavithra occupied chairs in Café coffee day

"Ms.Pavithra, we shall not handle this case directly by DC sir team because the accused will escape, so I will go with cops to Pune. Please come and join with us and prepare to go there, let us finish the case as soon as possible, more over I shall recommend to my senior about you to join our team " Ms.Sancheti

Ms.Pavithra eagerly asked "How many days I have to inform leave?"

CHAPTER SIX

Shot Two

Novatel Hotel.

"You look so pretty and fit" commented Ms.Sancheti to Ms.Pavithra while drinking high brewed coffee, added "Prepare quickly, we shall meet Wing Commander Mr.Harshwarthan now"

Ms.Sancheti told the cops in husky voice, "Bring Mr. Edwin to WC office"

/-

Mrs.Stella asked the cops," I have to talk with DC sir"

Cop called DC sir; they don't know what will happen hereafter.

"Sir, I and my daughter have to go for essential shopping. Will you please arrange?" asked Mrs.Stella.

"Ok madam, is it enough 2 hours for you?" asked Dc Mr.Somnath.

Skoda rapid picked up them from that private villa, gone to JP nagar central mall after rounded KSRTC lay-out.

They reached and the car was parked in ground parking area.

\-

Commanding office was seemed like head post office, broad parking area, parked army vehicles, surrounded with full of army uniformed cops.

Ms.Sancheti 's smart watch showed 10.50 AM when she was waiting in front of WC Mr.Harshwarthan's cabin and she was typing seriously regarding the scenes crossed in past couple of days.

/-

Mr.Soman's assistant called him, "Sir, I saw the persons 2 and 3 are here you mentioned on that day, I am waiting for your order to catch them.

"Ok, tell me the location, I will be there in minutes" said Mr.Soman with terror mind.

Mr.Soman took his old model Taurus revolver and gone to the location in a speed like a Jet.

\-

WC Mr.Harshwarthan was in his uniform and stood in a professional style and said "Welcome Ms.Sancheti, How are you? I think you came with a new project, am I right?" added "First sit and tell me what's the matter and narrate me how I can guide you?"

This is the way always he welcomes his juniors and delivers every word supporting.

He ordered coffee to Ms.Sancheti and the assistants went out from the scene.

Ms.Sancheti narrated the case simply.

After she finished Ms.Pavithra told her 3 calls missed in Sancheti's phone.

"With your permission" told Ms.Sancheti to call the missed number. Her face changed into serious mode when she got the information from her assistants.

/-

There was so busy and crowd in Central mall parking area. More number of cops was there.

Cops make path for ambulance. Someone shot Mrs.Stella and her daughter and they have fallen near DC sir car.

Ambulance assistants picked both Stella and her daughter and rushed.

"Both shot in safer places" said ambulance medical officer and gave injection for arrest bleeding, fix oxy mask for both of them" assistants done their duty.

Both Mrs.Stella and her daughter were shifted to another vehicle and rushed to Campbell hospital.

The car driver and the cop who came with Mrs.Stella were waken up from a dizzy mood and noticed that ambulance flown.

Cab driver called DC sir and tried to follow the ambulance. There was no chance the vehicle at GH road, as per the control room guidance and in minutes they found empty ambulance parked near BTM second stage.

/-

Mrs.Stella and her daughter were kept in ICU 2 of Campbell hospital. "DC sir, someone kept a mother and daughter in our hospital ICU, their conversations are suspicious and they have planned to shift them to somewhere after the bullets removed" said Ms.Reethu (Who was appointed as informer by DC Sir)

"Ok Ms.Reethu, make delay in formalities and my team will be there soon" said DC Mr.Somnath and added" whether both are safe?"

"No sir, Mother in safe condition but daughter in critical stage still" replied Ms.Reethu.

When Reethu enter into ICU 2, the ambulance accompanied doctors with half-filled blood bottles. She said to them "Chief doctor will come now"

"Sister, our Dean informed us to discharge both and bring there, we shall move after informing your chief doctor, ok?"

\-

Ms.Sancheti narrated everything to WC sir.

"Let us check any evidence available in Dr.KaliCharan's Hospital" said WC Mr.Harshwarthan. And added

"I will arrange to send both of you and Ms.Pavithra there"

Then he moved to attend an internal meeting.

Ms.Sancheti and Ms.Pavithra went to the navigator community room in WC office.

Mr.Edwin came out from dizzy mode, was in a corner of navigator room which part is covered with bullet proof glass seated in a chair without any knots.

Ms.Sancheti and Ms.Pavithra entered the room and sat near Mr.Edwin.

Ms.Sancheti took a flat device from her handbag and scanned both hands finger print of Mr.Edwin with that device and came out from that room without any conversation with Mr.Edwin.

\-

Ms.Pavithra called Ms.Nandhini "Do you need any help from me?"

"I didn't receive salary credit from company; shall you inform Mr.Jegan about this?" Nandhini asked.

"Ok I will inform him sure" Pavithra closed the call.

"It will take 2 hours to reach Mangalore after check in, shall we take food here?" asked Ms.Sancheti.

"Yes, I need to have" replied Ms.Pavithra

Both had consumed some dishes in South Indian Make-In counter. Ms.Pavithra done some shopping .

\-

DC Mr.Somnath formally informed IMA Head, Bangalore and sent to arrest the ambulance accompanied doctors. The cops brought them to DC office.

Campbell senior doctor gave report of Stella's daughter as good to move, the cops brought them to GH and admitted in special ward for observation and informed DC and Ms.Sancheti about they were in safe custody.

/-

Ms.Sancheti 's cab crossed the KPT Junction in Kadri park to AJHR road and turn right to reach KC Multi-speciality hospital. They entered and parked in parking lane 2 as guided by security.

After showing their ID card, they have informed to wait in lounge. Ms.Sancheti's and Ms.Pavithra's ID card perfectly created by WC team as they are coming from IMA, Bangalore.

Receptionist informed Dr.KaliCharan about their visit after confirming their appointment date and time.

"Madam, you may go to Dr.KaliCharan sir cabin" Said receptionist.

Ms.Sancheti and Ms.Pavithra went inside Dr.KaliCharan AC cabin. He showed his hands to sit in the chair. They both occupied.

Dr.KaliCharan was in navy blue safari suit, turned towards Ms.Sancheti and asked

"Tell me madam, are you from IMA?"

His rough voice changed suddenly to soft and cool after he saw Ms.Pavithra's smiling face.

"Sorry, I was in a tension" tried to make them cool.

"Its ok sir, There was a convention in IMA, next month. Our High official decided to fix you as Chief Guest. So please be prepared for that. We came to update your profile now. Ms.Sancheti replied.

Dr.KC turned towards Sancheti but a personal call interrupted him.

"Excuse me" told Dr.KC and went to attend the call.

"Sister, what happened to us, where are we now?' asked Mrs.Stella .

Nurse narrated simply and told them, soon they will go to home.

/-

Ms.Sancheti took some essential tools and basic safety devices for her and also Ms.Pavithra and entered in the registry of WC office Arms store.

\-

After Nandhini 's health improved, her mother prepared to go her own town near Pune. Nandhini went to send off her mother in Airport and came back her apartment; there were 2 missed calls from Pavithra.

Just formally asked about her mother, Ms.Pavithra said "Good night"

CHAPTER SEVEN

Trace Main

Inside Dr.KaliCharan's Cabin

That phone call was from IMA Joint secretary, "Good morning Mr.KC, How are you?, Your topic is the high light in forthcoming Convention meeting, I hope you will be the next IMA President of course, Congrats, and then please provide the details to our staffs. All the best" said and concluded.

Again a missed call but this was from his wife.

Replied in husky voice," Sweety, here an important guest meeting, shall I call you after a while?" put the phone.

Ms.Sancheti used the golden minutes.

She put a device adjacent to Dr.KC's laptop; it shows the desktop files in her apple phone. She selected one file and copy and paste.

She takes 2 visiting cards and pasted some gel in the surface of card.

She fixed a screw like device in the edge of vinyl particle rubber beading.

She asked Dr.KC's assistant a cup of water. He turned back she took 2 sheets from table pad.

She took a photo snap of the door keys hanged in Cabin door.

She inserted a nail like pin device in to the three pin socket near her seat.

Dr.KC came in and said"Excuse me, important calls to attend" and sat in his chair.

After few minutes, he gave the details to them.

Ms.Sancheti thanked him for the supportive conversation.

When they stand to came out, Dr.KC put two visiting cards on the table and saw silently Ms.Pavithra to take. Ms.Pavithra got it without touching the main surface of cards and put in to a poly bag for finger print safety.

Ms.Sancheti and Ms.Pavithra went to the car parking area, sat inside the cab, and said to cab driver to buy water bottle from nearby shop.

Ms.Sancheti opened her laptop, now they saw Dr.KC's cabin in clear live video. She pressed a device; colorless smoke came from the socket in KC's cabin. Slightly DR.KC went to dizzy mode. Ms.Pavithra ran little fast to that cabin and bring Dr.KC's mobile.

Meanwhile, Ms.Sancheti sent the available data taken from Dr.KC's laptop to Dc sir and WC sir.

This time Dr.KC's Finger print from visiting card used to open his mobile phone. The extra powered device connected with antenna sent more than 40GB data to WC sir system which collected from KC sir mobile phone.

Ms.Sancheti went to the receptionist, "Madam, we finished our appointment, but KC sir fallen down in dizzy mode, please come and see"

Sancheti ran into the cabin along with receptionist and placed KC's mobile phone in the Table as it is and came back. On the way she informed an assistant staff to go to KC sir cabin saying that receptionist calling her.

After she reached the cab they escaped quickly.

\-

WC Mr.Harshwarthan checked all the files and told Ms.Sancheti and Ms.Pavithra, "The matter is serious but if even we give these files to DC sir, he need perfect evidence to catch them. After I discuss with my senior and DC sir, we will come to a conclusion, ok?"

And added

"Meanwhile please take lunch in our canteen now"

/-

Dr.Amrinthar and Dr.Jacob both near Dr.KC's Bed

"How do you feel now, Mr.KC and what happen to you?" asked Dr.Jacob.

Dr.KC replied "Nothing, just dizziness"

Dr.KC asked the receptionist "Have you verified the IMA guys ID before allowing them inside?"

"Yes sir verified" receptionist replied with some fear.

"It's ok, I am ok and nothing to worry, you both may go and we shall meet you in bar evening." Dr.KC replied to both doctors firmly.

Dr.KC went to his home and taken rest for some hours.

\-

By using both Edwin and KaliCharan's finger prints,Ms.Sancheti inspected their bank lockers, she found the following in Mr.Edwin's

1. Building document of a Multiplex complex near Hussain Sagar Lake at Hyderabad.

And Mr.KC's

1. A gold embossed Gaddafi Model gun.
2. 3 million US dollors.

/-

"Ms.Sancheti, we cannot move further with now available proof. I have informed DC.Somnath sir to put cops in various spots around KC's area. If any strong evidence traced against Dr.KC's team, we can lock them in a case, let's wait and see"

Ms.Sancheti called the research team head in WC office and asked "Any evidence available through paper mapping?"

"Yes madam, one phone number" Replied Team Head.

Found from unwritten papers taken by Ms.Sancheti from KC sir cabin.

She took her mobile phone and typed the said number; it shows the name of that number through True caller app.

Name: Stella Edwin.

On regular meeting held in Army officers, they discussed about the rescue accessories and new electronic devices to protect every women herself in critic situations.

And also one army personnel undergone a major operation in Army Hospital and suddenly they searched for the rare blood group for that operation.

After severe search they found a private hospital supplying that group blood. They paid huge amount for two bottles of blood.

WC Mr.Harshwarthan collected the contact number of that private hospital for future references.

\-

"Ms.Pavithra, right now we are going to conduct an operation called "Operation Red steals"Be prepare in 2 minutes". Said Ms.Sancheti in a hurry.

Ms.Sancheti's cab turns right after KPT Junction in Airport road. There they found Dr.KC's car is going in front of Sancheti's cab.

They speed up and blocked Dr.KC's car near KPT ITI college.

Masked guys get down and showed their gun towards Dr.KC and sprayed in his face to get dizzy and the same to driver also. Both were picked up and went to Army base hospital.

Ms.sancheti called KC sir Wife "madam, KC sir suddenly got illness; we have sent you a car to pick up. Don't get nervous, we shall take care, please come"

Cops kept both Dr.KC and his wife in separate ward and put injection to sleep to both.

Sancheti rushed fast with Pavithra and her team mates to Dr.KaliCharan's house for inspection.

/-

Nandhini called "Ms.Pavithra, when will you come back? I feel so weak."

Pavithra replied "Soon my friend, tell me what's your blood group?" heard her group and shocked.

\-

Dr.KC's wife came to hospital murmured KC sir name often on the way she travelled. She is a Bp patient so the sister kept them in a separate room. After checking her Bp level the sister put an injection mentioned by WC sir. She went to dizzy mode in the seat itself.

Sister and assistants put her on a bed and waited for Ms.Sancheti's next phone call

After inspection by Ms.Sancheti and her team was over, the cops shifted both Dr.KC and her wife to their home bedroom and came out of the scene and informed Ms.Sancheti.

Wc Mr.Harshwarthan asked Ms.Sancheti "Why so soon you hijacked Dr.KC and his wife?"

"No sir if the news leaked the case will be so weak and not able to move fast. And sorry for the action, if it's wrong timed one" replied Ms.Sancheti.

/-

Inspection scene...

Ms.Sancheti and Pavithra searched nook and corner of DR.KC sir house,

They found jewels and some US dollors only. After four hours of search, they ready to back up and came out of the house.

/-

When Ms.Nandhini went for checkup and for treatment at Dr.Ashok clinic, her blood was stolen from her body without her knowledge. It's rare group blood.

\-

Dr.KaliCharan and Dr.Jacob gathered in KC sir cabin.

"Whether the Surgery we planned for the Emirate VIP patient was confirmed?"

"A small change, the donor already arranged was missed but I have arranged another donor also perfectly matched to the Emirate VIP" Jacob replied.

"Please confirm with Anesthetist. We have to do the surgery 100 percent success" said Dr.KC and started to move from there.

"Ok sir" and added "10 million bucks, single payment, came already from Emirate's account" Jacob and KC went out with happy mood.

Ms.Sancheti got the calling reports of Mr.Edwin and Dr.KC. There was an international phone number also in that report.

CHAPTER EIGHT

Liquid Gold

Inspection scene, once again.

When Ms.Sancheti and her team mates came out of Dr.KC sir house, Ms.Pavithra told “Madam, shall we check the car shed also?”

They all once again entered the car shed

It was spacious three car garage. One old model Ambassador MYX 1976 only was there in a corner. They check everywhere but no clue was there. When they prepare to came out, Ms.Pavithra showed Ms.Sancheti, “Madam, See here” the red color, 4 x 4 size floor mat was under the ambassador car.

They with the cops shifted the car and removed the mat. There they found old unused water tank. They removed the lid and there found inside four suitcases tied by rope with step ring.

They took all suitcases in their cab and placed the mat and the car as it is, then flown.

WC Mr.Harshwarthan received a call.” Sir, on Panvel-Kochi highway a young girl patient was shifted from a BMW to an ambulance. They seem to be suspicious and we hold them. We have sent you an image. Please check and inform what we have to do next” Cops from DC office asked.

WC sir opened the image, found the BMW number then sent it to control room to find out the owner of the car.

The BMW was in the name of Mr.Jacob.

“Shift the girl to Army base hospital, collect the current status of the patient, take BMW and the driver into our custody fast” WC.Mr.Harshwarthan command them.

/-

There were the patients reports, Organ donor agreements, ECG,EEG and scan reports along with research thesis files in the suitcases. The research team officers scrutinized them collect some important papers and put in court procedure file. They put the suitcases in the water tank, placed the floor mat and the car in the garage as it is.

When they went to Dr.KC sir house with suitcases, they also shifted DR.Kalicharan and his wife in dizzy mode and they placed both in their bedroom.

After hurry filled daytime work schedule, Ms.Pavithra slept with Ms.Sancheti after took some food.

Pavithra remembered and told to Ms.Sancheti that Dr.KaliCharan spelled several times the name of Mr.Jacob when they were in KC sir cabin.

"Ok Ms.Pavithra, search the contents collected from KC sir and find his friend's list" said Ms.Sancheti.

Ms.Sancheti called Dr.Kurian about the patient report of whom shifted from BMW.

"Madam, her name is Arthi, age 22. She has undergone in an organ transplant surgery, I am very much upset, please come and I will explain" Dr.Kurian replied sadly.

Ms.Sancheti got tensed.

\-

Dr.KaliCharan woke up from bed and thought what happened to him and asked himself , any dream saw yesterday.

He checked all over his home, nothing was missed. After had a coffee he remembers one by one.

He can't assume who was that mask covered guys and for what purpose they have done like this.

\-

A private charter flight is ready to take off from Mangalore terminal.

"Please convey our thanks to his highness Sultan, Madam, Do you feel everything comfort to your highness?" Dr,Jacob asked

The Queen of Emirates happily shaken hands to Dr.Jacob and smiled to say everything was going fine.

After all formalities over, The Queen and their 9 associate members went by.

Dr.Jacob came out of the Air launch pad, called to his driver, but the phone ring goes continuously but not picked. Then he took an UBER cab and went to hospital.

When he reaches there, Dr.Amrinthar got down from another cab and his face was in a serious mode.

\-

"Ms.Sancheti, Our DC sir team members collected one evidence, very good, now we have to call DC sir immediately to take action and prepare to file a supportive document at District Magistrate's court" and added " I informed DC sir to keep his crew in 10 spots again for if any strong evidence available more than this" said WC Mr.Harshwarthan .

Ms.Pavithra interfered "whether the available proof is not enough for issue a non-bail able warrant against them?"

He replied "No madam, they are fully professionals and if IMA support them, it's a shame for us" told and went by the department vehicle for an important inspection work.

Pavithra accepted his word.

\-

"Tell me darling, where we have to go now?" asked Dr.Amrinthar to his P.A. Ms.Jasmin das seated near him in his car.

(Ms.Jasmin das has finished M.Sc. Nursing in Dev Bhoomi Group of colleges, navgoen, Dehradun and got top rank in 2016 batch)

She replied "Bheema Jewellers" in a soft and husky voice.

The passengers going to exit way from UAE flight which came from DOHA of emirates, one well dressed guy looks like an ambassador of Rabon Rado company, came near his name written hand board and showed his hands towards Dr.Jacob's car driver.

The name written hand board spells "Robert Monton"

Dr.Jacob asked" Have you dropped Dr.Monton in Novatel suite safely? Driver replied "Yes Sir"

"Are you safe landed Doctor?" Dr.Jacob asked DR.Monton

"Yes Mister" Monton replied tiredly.

"Ok Doctor, We shall meet at Barcelona bar by evening, Take rest and refresh yourself"

\-

Dr.KC 's guest house was on the way to Tagore Park 100 feet after the Toyoto show room.

Dr.KaliCharan, Dr.Jacob and Dr.Amrinthar all three was seated in sofa in the front hall of the guest house. The hall was in pin drop silence.

Dr.KC breaks the silence and asked "Do you both feel any difference in the current life?"

"No Dr, why are you asking like this?" Jacob replied with question feel

"What happened to your patient Ms.Arthi?"

"I got a message from Ms.Arthi's phone as she reached home, Why any problem with her? Who told about her?" Dr.Jacob replied and added that his ambulance driver went on leave for 15 days and his BMW driver coming as usual.

Again Dr.Jacob asked "Any problem?"

KC replied as "My client noticed that a police vehicle cross examined your BMW, so that I asked you.

"Are you saying that whether police smelled our activities?" Dr.Jacob.

"I enquired but believable information came that there was no actions prosecuted yet." Dr.KC.

Then he turned towards Dr.Amrinthar "Why you are in a silent mode?"

"I feel and assume someone trace my phone calls?" said DR.Amrinthar.

"Ok let us handle everything after the meeting with Dr.Monton over"

Said Dr,KC and departed from there.

\-

Ms.Sancheti and Ms.Pavithra entered the Army base hospital to get the reports of Ms.Arthi.

Dr.Kurian narrated the report. Ms.Pavithra suddenly shocked after heard the narration.

“Is it true?” Ms.Sancheti also asked.

“Yes madam I am not able to digest, whether if it is possible then what was the future life of Ms.Arthi.

Dr.Kurian added “At present there is no doctor will take such a risk and illegal work to do”.

/-

In WC sir room,

“Madam, communication proof, organ theft proof, mode of transplant, illegal money everything ok, but to whom the surgery made, we have to find out soon” WC Harswarthan asked Ms.Sancheti.

“If I get permission from IMA, I can collect the details of organ transplant surgery done in this month, that please arrange me sir “said Ms.Sancheti

“Yes I will” WC sir replied and suddenly he called the Hospital once he saved in his phone from whom the rare group blood supplied.

\-

Dr.KaliCharan called to Mrs.Stella’s phone

“Mrs.Stella, Mr.Edwin sir Phone not reachable, what happened to him, where are you all now?” Dr.KaliCharan called to Mrs.Stella even though he know very well that the call may be traced by control room, as he want to know where Mr.Edwin was kept.

Mrs.Stella replied “He had some health issues, so he was admitted in hospital and we are within the same hospital in Pune, do you want to talk with him now?

“No no, tell him to call me after he is back in form” said Dr.KC and put the phone.

“Did I communicate with Dr.KC in correct way madam?” Pavithra asked Ms.Sancheti.

"Perfectly "said Ms.Sancheti and added "Whether Both Mrs.Stella and her daughter were safe and stayed in your control?"

"Yes, madam" Pavithra replied.

/-

Ms.Sancheti and Ms.Pavithra were in WC sir cabin.

"I have sorted 14 names that matched to Ms.Arthi's blood group, Out of which two patients closely to the date and time of the date we caught Ms.Arthi. One of them was a retired Electoral officer and another one was the Queen of his highness Sultan of Arab Emirates.

As per the report given by Dr.Kurian, was perfectly matching to that Queen Sir. Ms.Sancheti explained to WC Harshwarthan.

At once, WC Harshwarthan called the Embassy of UAE, and asked 7 day patient transfer list.

Crime records room in-charge of DC sir office, informed Ms.Sancheti about a call received for the assistant Mr.John Britto's mobile phone of which was kept in records room.

Ms.Sancheti told to trace the call with the help of control room.

Ms.Nandhini called Ms.Pavithra" how many days will take to finish your project, my friend?

"I will come in fortnight, Ms.Nandhini, How is your health now, your blood illegally taken from your body when you were admitted in Dr.Ashok sir clinic, so take extra care on your health. Don't worry, you will resume soon. Take some nutritional tonic daily.

Added,"I will sure attend your marriage function, ok?" Ms.Pavithra replied.

\-

Ms.Sancheti got a message from control room. They searched and found the missed call came for Dr.Ashok sir assistant Mr.John Britto was An Insurance broker.

CHAPTER NINE

Story Start

Irwin Auditorium, spruce street, Philadelphia.

It was the year 1999, winter exposed chill filled roads.

The venue filled with 40 medical students with hot air jerkins along with seniors and computer operators to register the venue recordings waiting for the research scholars for delivering their historical thesis.

Building manager inspected everything in and around the building and went to his office room.

They, Dr.KaliCharan and Dr.Jacob got down from "Mustang" of Ford which escorted with ordinary RR cars.

Dr.KaliCharan and his Desk mate Dr.Jacob were gone to the stage and started to deliver their Historical thesis reports.

Dr.Jacob delivered the new possibilities in intravenous handling in major surgery. Everyone claps for the excellent narration.

Dr.KaliCharan delivered his thesis in the topic for the futuristic need and possible 21'st century methods in Organ Transplant surgery.

The venue was in pin drop silence for few minutes, slowly everyone of the venue gave him a standing ovation for his extraordinary research and astonished by clapping for continuous ten minutes.

\-

"Ms.Sancheti, I got the patients transfer data" said WC Mr.Harshwarthan.

/-

It was January 2017, winter started to close its wings.

There was Dr.KaliCharan, Dr.Jacob with co working Doctors, important Medical professionals of Dr.KC Multi-specialty Hospital gathered in an Air-conditioned banquet hall.

Dr.KaliCharan explained his success on Organ transplant surgery after 18 years of struggle. It was possible now with the help of Artificial Intelligence. This party is to celebrate that victory in human testing.

Midnight Bistro Restaurant was filled with joy and the cling sounds of bottles.

\-

Ms.Sancheti explained the introduction and usage of new age personal weapons to Ms.Pavithra on the website of Arms and Ammunitions department.

They both got flurry when the call came from WC sir.

\-

That was April 2017

Dr.KaliCharan called "Dear Jacob, we shall meet in the same ball room tonight. Inform Dr Amrinthar also"

Dr.Jacob knows the reason for the party because he also accompanied the major surgery with Dr.KaliCharan.

They both know very well IMA will not give approval for this critical surgery as it is life or death risk for the patient receiving the organ.

But money makes every man slave. If it's goldmine the mind will do anything.

It's first time Dr.KaliCharan doing this surgery and no one has the talent as well as the courage he has. So billionaires in India and abroad, waiting for his appointment.

/-

To clarify herself, Ms.Sancheti asked WC Harshwarthan, "Whether by the way of BMW and Ambulance drivers shall our actions smelled by KC and team?"

"No madam, within ten minutes we caught Ms.Arthi, I have inserted a signal device in Ms.Arthi's body while she was in dizzy mode and I request apology to the both drivers regarding we got a wrong information so we have interrupted them and sent back both on their own route." And added

"After Ms.Arthi reached safely in her home, I have sent a team to her house, for taking her once again, as she need a MRI scan to give her speedy recovery injections, our team brought her to our Army base hospital. Now her family members are there with her.

\-

"As per my informer,The foreigner stayed in Novatel Hotel is going to meet Dr.KC sir team tonight, please prepare and get a list of Ball room booking members " WC sir said and added " Inform DC sir to be prepare to make a formal visit to Novatel Hotel with custom papers"

/-

"Ms.Nandhini, we got a reminder call and a formal message about your Insurance payment was unpaid still date. What happen to you?" asked the Team Head Mr.Jegan.

Ms.Nandhini replied "No sir, I am paying all dues in time and I will check once again sir"

\-

"Mr.Amrinthar, your cheque was not cleared and unpaid for the jewels purchased. Will you please make it settle soon?" asked an officer from Bheema jewellers.

At once Dr.Amrinthar called his Clinic accountant to check the bank balance and to clear the issue immediately.

/-

"Sorry Mr.KaliCharan, someone smelled my visit and particularly our meeting, I hereby cancel my program and going back to my country Bye" informed Dr.Monton and closed the call without hearing his reply.

The luxury car picked Dr.Robert Monton and went towards Airport.

\-

After she checked the letter and email came from Insurance Company, Ms.Nandhini was shocked and at once called

Ms.Pavithra. The policy sum assured value was ten million. Ms.Pavithra told her to forward the mail to her.

/-

WC office.

The assistant called WC "Sir, one emergency ticket booked to Toronto from Novatel Air booking desk. Shall we search and hold the passenger?"

"No need, you just collect the available details of the passenger and send me by email" said WC Harshwarthan.

\-

Accountant informed Dr.Amrinthar

"We got a mail from our bank that Our clinic business account as well as your personal account was freezed. I will call the Bank manager".

When he asked the Bank manager he directed the call to Section A.M

The section A.M replied "Sir Dr.Amrinthar sir account freezed by their high official in Head office. Please send us a written request to our bank address or otherwise tell the Dr to come and meet our BM.

/-

Ms.Pavithra read the mail forwarded from Ms.Nandhini. She remembered some where she saw the name of Insurance Company. Suddenly she took Ms.Arthi's file, she found that the same amount insured, the same Company.

She informed Ms.Sancheti about this and as per her guidance she called the local branch head of that insurance company, " Will you please provide me the name of the person or DSA who initiate the Policy given number?" they gave the details only after she mention WC sir.

\-

"Ms.Sancheti, here you have news that the person stayed in Novatel Hotel that day was an Interpol officer" said WC Harshwarthan

" Dr.Monton was a suspicious criminal searched by Interpol team. To know their Network in India, Interpol team blocked and kept him in cell and instead of him an officer came to India in Monton's ticket.When he knows our speed of investigation, he returned to Toronto for not giving confusion to our work. This information I got from their office in charge" narrated WC Harshwarthan to Ms.Sancheti and added "You and Ms.Pavithra go to DC office and cooperate him to speed up and catch everyone involved in this case and update me often" WC sir moved out .

Ms.Pavithra informed Ms.Sancheti "Madam I found both Ms.Nandhini and Ms.Arthi insurance cover initiated by Dr.Ashok"

\-

Dc.Somnath called "Ms.Sancheti, I have created a case file against Mr.Edwin with both criminal and civil two cases each, whether you have any suggestion of adding any?"

Ms.Sancheti "No sir, it's enough, you please carry on" and turned to Ms.Pavithra,

"Ms.Pavithra I will arrange you some important case files from DC sir. You just go through it. It will be very useful to follow the future cases you deal with"

Ms.Sancheti said to WC sir "For Dr.KC sir case clarification I am going to meet Mr.Edwin and update you soon sir"

After communicated with Mr.John about insurance initiated by Dr.Ashok ,Ms.Sancheti called and requested DC sir

"Dc sir, please file a separate case on Mr.John as murder trial on Ms.Nandhini "

\-

Team Head Mr.Jegan called

"Ms.Pavithra, you have taken leave more days for your personal work,

Please give us explanation letter regarding why we should not take department wise action against you" and added

"We expect from you soon and date of back to office reporting also"

Ms.Pavithra replied "Yes certainly mail to you, sir"

CHAPTER TEN

Safe Escape

Morning 05.30.

Officials entered into.

"Dr.Amrinthar, we are from IT wing Vigilance department, we have to search your belongings, kindly support us"

Dr.Amrinthar shocked, sat in sofa and showed hands silently to carry on.

\-

"Ms.Sancheti, I am very much interested to work with you, there was pressure to came back to work in my office, shall I resign and join with your team?" Ms.Pavithra asked eagerly.

"No, Ms.Pavithra, already I have sent your profile to our head office, they will sure confirm soon. You have to pass a written test and undergo 90-120 day training probably in Dehradun or Wellington" and added

"You just your finish your formalities in your job to resign and attend your friend Ms.Nandhini's marriage and let's work with" replied Ms.Sancheti and gone to DC office with Ms.Pavithra.

"Ms.Nandhini, I have read your mail regarding the Insurance. I have checked with their regional office. We shall cancel the policy within the pre-look period with the hands of the person initiated that policy. Don't worry my friend be cool and enjoy the sweet fear of forthcoming marriage, OK?"

Ms.Pavithra and booked tickets to attend her marriage after getting the date from Ms.Nandhini.

Dc sir got all the evidences of money transfer and documents related to the illegal surgery from the IT wing on request.

Dc.Somnath sir thanked Ms.Jasmine das for the support given by her for tracking Dr.Amrinthar's activities.

\-

A chip for tracing signals was injected in the back neck of Dr.Monton in the name of medical checkup and released by Interpol to find out his back support and informed to WC sir.

/-

Crime records room in-charge of DC sir office called Ms.Sancheti and gave all the materials and belongings of Mr.Edwin.

Wallet, car key, mobile phone and smart watch were there. Ms.Sancheti called the hacker to transfer all the data to her tab.

One particular 4-digit number mentioned in smart watch disturbed her mind. That's "1976". She shows the number to Ms.Pavithra. Ms.Pavithra has excellent brain suitable for Army training. Suddenly she said "Madam, the number belongs to Dr.Kc sir old Ambassador Car"

\-

Ms.Pavithra called Team Head Mr.Jegan "Sir, I have decided to resign from our company and I will send the formal confirmation mail to you"

"Are you sure Ms.Pavithra?" Mr.Jegan asked.

"Yes sir, it is confirmed" replied Ms.Pavithra.

"Then ok, I will forward your confirmation mail to our head office, wishes to you" said Mr.Jegan formally

\-

DC sir got search warrant from DM for checking Dr.KC sir house, farm house, guest house and his hospital very particularly the Ambassador car, in addition to check all his team members and friends.

He sent some team of cops to search entire places connected with Dr.KC.

/-

Nandhini's mother called" Ms.Pavithra, groom's family confirmed the marriage date and printed invitations also. I will send one for you. At least you must be here to accompany and coordinate our family one week before, ok?"

"Yes of course mom, with pleasure" Pavithra replied.

When cops went to search Dr.KC sir house, Ms.Sancheti and Ms.Pavithra also accompanied with them.

When they came to garage, three more cops and Ms.Sancheti madam searched thoroughly the Ambassador. They can't find anything from there. The historical 'Cling" sound Ms.Pavithra heard when she opened the backside door of that car. The sound wakens up Pavithra's brain.

Ms.Sancheti told the cops to separate the door apart.

Dc sir asked Ms.Sancheti "Any particular clue available there?"

"DC sir, please come at once here" her voice said a lot.

Ms.Sancheti called WC Mr.Harshwarthan' Sir, an excellent cadre you have got for your preferential team" she narrated about Ms.Pavithra found the great discovery in the car.

DC Somnath came and rounded the car. Ms.Sancheti showed one particular spot. He said "Wow"

And asked her "who found this?"

Ms.Sancheti told "The credit goes to Ms.Pavithra" and turned to show Ms.Pavithra but she is not there.

Ms.Sancheti searched her by calling her name but she was not there.

She called Ms.Pavithra by phone, ring goes, but not picked by her

/-

Dr.KaliCharan, Dr.Jacob and Dr Amrinthar were arrested by Cops accompanied by DC.Somnath and they all were kept in separate cabins for interrogation.

\-

The bouncers connected with Dr.KC team followed Ms.Sancheti and Ms.Pavithra and parked some visible distance from KC sir house. When Ms.Sancheti busy in her work, Ms.Pavithra came out to attend a call near entrance gate of KC sir house, they the bouncers went near back side of Ms.Pavithra and caught by covering her mouth by palm for not making noise and shifted to their car then ran out of the scene.

A call from a new number disturbed Ms.Sancheti,

"Please bring all evidences related to KC sir and team, submit all of them in KC sir Hospital. Then we release Ms.Pavithra" call gone silent.

"Cops go and search Ms.Pavithra, I will inform control room to guide you" DC sir said.

Ms.Sancheti asked WC sir help.

/-

The bouncers sealed Ms.Pavithra's mouth with plasters and seated left and right to her. The car ran fast in Airport road.

Suddenly Ms.Pavithra showed abnormal fear in her eyes and saw both of them to see her feet as seemed something was there. Both of them bend towards her feet.

/-

"White pretty gown, dark color shorts, coffee brown overcoat, name Ms.Pavithra, Age 25, I have sent her image in whatsapp, search all out going roads from the location mentioned, check every vehicle, go fast" commanded DC sir.

\-

Wc.Harshwarthan sent a mini copter, 4 drone directors to search around the location shared by Ms.Sancheti.

After the bouncers bend to the right position Ms.Pavithra pressed a bubble like device in her wrist towards the bouncers. Perfect shot reach them. They both went to dizzy mode.

Ms.Pavithra removed her mouth plasters; beat the driver with her gun. She opened the right side door and pushed the bouncer and also she used him as wheel chair, she flown out.

The car rolled towards left of roadside.

The drone came towards the Airport road showed her location to its director. He picked her and went back to KC sir house.

After a little breath, Ms.pavithra called Ms.Sancheti "Madam, I am safe"

"Thank you Ms.Pavithra, I hope you will manage yourself, even though I have to arrange the force for you" said Ms.Sancheti and informed WC sir with an official thanks.

Ms.Sancheti told to Ms.Pavithra "Your findings was the hot topic of this hour Ms.Pavithra, and this message rounds all over the department from DGP to WC and added "Come fast to the spot"

Dc Mr.Somnath rushed to his office with all evidence materials.

In DC office,

IMA state president called DC sir and asked "Good evening sir, shall you able to narrate the present case filed on KC sir in simple words?"

DC Somnath sir shortly described the case and added "its non-bail able offence, so we need your cooperation please"

"Oh, sure" the President replied.

\-

After Ms.Pavithra reached the spot, Ms.Sancheti came to her and gave a welcome hug and told "You are the main reason to collect this historic evidence and with your self-protecting talent, you came out from a critic crime scene. This incident is enough to approve your application for joining our team. Well done" said Ms.Sancheti and brought her to the Ambassador.

"Wow" Ms.Pavithra got excited.

The doors of that Ambassador was separated and opened. There were more evidences like pen drive, discs and lots of documents. The secret of Ambassador was also disclosed.

CHAPTER ELEVEN

Bird Flown

Mrs.Stella called Ms.Sancheti

"Madam I have a request from you"

“Yes tell me madam” Sancheti.

“I have advised several times to Mr.Edwin for not support the KC sir team, he never valued my words. Will you please allow me to talk with him? My lawyer said if he changed his mind he can made him as approver for this case. Shall you please madam?” she seems to cry.

“Is he obeying your words at present situation?” asked Ms.Sancheti.

“Yes, madam I will narrate him about my daughter’s future and he shall obey now” said Mrs.Stella.

Ms.Sancheti showed the secret of Ambassador.

Ms.Pavithra asked “How you find out the secret?”

Ms.Sancheti showed an old photo taken out of the documents from door. And said “This photo was taken when the old ambassador car done tinkering work un-finished stage”

But Ms.Pavithra asked “This is also the same ambassador?”

“No. go through the basic frame style, it is vary from the original”

“Excellent Ms.Pavithra, the same difference I have noticed” and she took a tool and scratched in a small area of the door that is amazing!

The door and main accessories made out of 18 carat gold. They made as old ambassador car model with some changes.

Ms.Sancheti saw Ms.Pavithra with proud.

\-

Dc.Somnath filed civil and criminal cases against Dr.KaliCharan and his team members. He collected and sorted all the documents and evidences to submit to the court. Ms,Sancheti and Ms.Pavithra helped him very much on that table work.

/-

Team Head Mr.Jegan helped Ms.Pavithra to get the releasing order after checking all her accounts; the company will issue the settlement amount soon to her account.

Ms.Pavithra thanked him for the help.

Ms.Nandhini applied for a long leave for her marriage.

\-

DC sir arranged a party to WC sir and his team mates for rendering their valuable working hours allocating to his department services.

He thanked WC Harshwarthan sir and Ms.Sancheti on that party

Ms.Sancheti called "Ms.Pavithra, please join with us to the party"

"Why madam, is it necessary?" asked Ms.Pavithra.

No Ms.Pavithra, it is a professional protocol. You must know everything about this culture. You will find more officers to get intro also"

Then She said "Yes, Madam"

WC Harshwarthan enclosed his recommendation letter for the joining and training approval for Ms.Pavithra.

/-

Ms.Pavithra whole heartedly thanked Ms.Sancheti for providing exclusive personal safety devices to her from Army weapon stores by getting special permission from WC sir.

\-

"Ms.Sancheti madam, you must attend my marriage" Asked Nandhini

Ms.Pavithra also compelled Ms.Sancheti

"Sorry my friends, I have lots of reports to prepare and to submit in time and my vacation period almost over due to this case, I have to spend little time with my family before joining duty. But sure one fine day I will visit your house with Ms.Pavithra. Okay?" Ms.Sancheti refused very softly.

/-

New Jersey, Stephen's College.

Weapons Engineering department was decorated with miniature lamps.

After studies over, Ms.Pavithra called by the department , for Farewell Party.

She interacts with old class mates, professors and hostel in-charge.

She enjoyed the day with friends and rounded the town also. She made some shopping particularly Gifts for Nandhini.

When she was prepared to come back, her friends felt so much and no interest to go home.

She went for check-in at the counter and got the luggage slip and prepared to wait more than 90 minutes until her flight came.

Ms.Nandhini sent a whatsapp message."Where are you? Have you started?"

She made a whatsapp call to Nandhini"I am at waiting lounge Ms.Nandhini, reach there soon"

"Congratulations Ms.Pavithra, your application got approved" whatsapp message from Ms.Sancheti.

A forward message from WC Mr.Harshwarthan,

"The Project Organ you have done with Ms.Sancheti was very good. We hope that soon you will join our team to serve the nation". The message was received from the High Commands.

Mrs.Stella thanked Ms.Sancheti for admitting Mr.Edwin as approver. Ms.Sancheti informed Ms.Pavithra about this.

Ms.Pavithra eats some south Indian food and again came to waiting lounge. An old lady crossed suddenly with her luggage and un-expectedly. Ms.Pavithra fell down. Strong Male hands caught her shoulder and make her balanced.

“Thank you mister” said Ms.Pavithra and tries to see his face.

She relaxed in waiting chair. He vanished by saying “Bye” to her.

\-

Mr.Dyanesh reddy, Hyderabad DSP called Ms.Sancheti,

“Madam with your kind information we have suspended Mr.Nithin and his mate for doing favor to the criminal persons, Thank you”

She called and gave suggestion to the IT wing vigilance department for auditing and inspecting Dr.KaliCharan regarding the Golden Ambassador.

/-

IMA issued a note in their Medical Bulletin as they de-bar Mr.KaliCharan and team temperorily.

IMA Presidant tweeted as they will take necessary action on Dr.KaliCharan and his team.

WC Harshwarthan arranged a mini party in his department for Ms.Pavithra for her training approval and introduced their department staffs.

Ms.Sancheti happily congratulated Ms.Pavithra and Gift her parcel.

Ms.Pavithra opened the parcel.

“Brand new Magnum Research BFR personal revolver with its registered and quality assurance certificate”

Ms.Pavithra hugged Ms.Sancheti for the great honor she gave to her.

/-

Before she started to move for Ms.Nandhini’s Marriage, WC harshwarthan called her.

“Ms.Pavithra, I will give you a project simultaneously you can do along with your training , to support you I will arrange a laptop on my own risk that you please collect from the Army stores” Said and gave a cover to her.

\-

Nandhini’s marriage was simply arranged in her own town near Pune.

Ms.Nandhini introduced Ms.Pavithra to her husband and her family members.

Ms.Pavithra gave a gift to her and wished her whole heartedly.

\-

The famous lawyer Mr.Athiseshan argued for Dr.KaliCharan as under:

"Dr.Kalicharan not involved directly in this case my lord, There is no evidence against him as

1. His signature not seen in any surgery report
2. For illegal money or any case related to civil he shall submit suitable documents from his auditor.

So he is eligible to apply for bail with your kind permission.

So easily Mr.KaliCharan got bail from this case.

On second day with his strong friends background Dr.KaliCharan flown to Philadelphia to meet his friends.

Dr.Jacob and Dr.Amrinthar were put on non bail-able case and locked in remand

/-

There was Dr.Robert Monton's photo and his details in the cover WC sir gave to Ms.Pavithra. And alsohe gave some important devices to use for the project.

An approval letter for Army training at Dehradun was also there in cover.

\-

Ms.Sancheti started to Haldwani of Nainital District to spend his time with her family for a week.

Ms.Pavithra came to send off her and informed about the project WC sir gave her.

Ms.Sancheti assured her she will be joined in her team after she finished the formal training.

/-

The court ordered Dr.Jacob to give interim subsidy of 2 million bucks to the Patient Ms.Arthi.

\-

Ms.Pavithra informed her apartment owner that she is going for six month training and she added after that she need the same for her.

The Owner requested her to store her belongings in a separate room and to permit him until then he want to use that apartment as 'service apartment'

She said "Yes Sir, please"

/-

Ms.Pavithra packed her things and called the Cab.

She took her luggage and her vanity bag and got down by lift and wait for cab near his apartment entrance gate.

Suddenly a Honda bike came near. A young guy asked her

"Halo madam, How are you?"

"You mister?" asked Ms.Pavithra.

"I helped you in Airport lounge, do you remember me?"

And added "Shall I help you now?"

"No, no, I have booked cab and it will come soon, Thank you" she replied.

"Ok madam, this is my card, you may call me any time " Said that guy and gave two cards from his wallet and started to go.

She read the name in that card

"Dr.Vivek Raja Rathnan. M.B.B.S., DO."

Her mind thought

"Oh My God, Again from square one?"

THE END

My Books

My first English novel launched as E-book and as well as Paperback edition in United States market by Amazon on 24th March 2022

My second novel (Tamil) submitted to Kannadasan Pathippagam on 14th April 2022 for publishing

My third English novel published by <notionpress.com> on 2nd July 2022

My next novels on process were:

Judgement Gothic-the MAN

MicRrone-The adverse effects.

9 798887 721538

Printed by Libri Plureos GmbH in Hamburg, Germany